MY MOMMA
LIKES TO SAY

By DENISE BRENNAN-NELSON

Illustrated by JANE MONROE DONOVAN

*To my momma, for all the funny, odd
and special things you say to me.*

*And to Rebecca and Rachel,
"keep a song in your heart!"*

Denise

*Thanks to my parents for all of their
love and support, and for teaching me that
"a picture is worth a thousand words."*

Jane

Sleeping Bear Press™

2395 South Huron Parkway
Suite 200
Ann Arbor, MI 48104
www.sleepingbearpress.com

Printed and bound in the United States.

15 14 13 12

Library of Congress Cataloging-in-Publication Data
Brennan-Nelson, Denise.
My momma likes to say / written by Denise Brennan-Nelson;
illustrated by Jane Donovan.
p. cm.
ISBN 978-1-58536-106-9
1. English language-Idioms. 2. Children-Language. 3. Figures of speech.
4. Proverbs, English. 5. Parent and child. 6. Clichés. 7. Maxims. I. Title.
PE1462.B74 2003
398.9'21—dc21   2003002194

Introduction

When I was a little girl my momma had a lot of funny expressions that she liked to say to me. For example, *keep your eyes peeled*. She was asking me to be alert and help her find something while I was imagining peeling my eyes like a banana!

I know these expressions have names like maxims, idioms, proverbs, and clichés. There are thousands of them in the English language and they come from many different sources. They can be confusing, but fun, and are an important part of our language.

Eventually we learn the meanings of the many expressions that are used. Some of them are said so often—*catch you later*—that they become clichés. Others are full of wisdom and simple truths, such as *you can't judge a book by its cover*, and they provide some of life's most valuable lessons. You might want to keep track of some of those special phrases your momma says to you and see what you can learn from them!

To parents: Someday your children will recall and repeat the sweet, quirky expressions that you say to them. Before they discover their real meanings, think of all the delightful interpretations they can create in their minds. Imagine what they think when you sit down next to them, look them straight in the eye and say, "I'm all ears."

Does your momma ever say things
that you think are quite amusing?
Does your momma ever say things
that you find a bit confusing?

My momma says some funny things
like, "You're as sweet as pie,"
"Be as good as gold," and "You're the apple of my eye."

Sometimes I'm not sure
what momma's words mean.
But I really love the way
she whispers, "sweet dreams."

I wonder if my momma knows
how much I love her words.
She says a lot of special things
though some are just absurd!

Many years ago the pupil of the eye was thought to be
shaped like an apple. The pupil or "apple" of the eye was
precious because without it, you couldn't see.

When your momma says this to you, it means you are
very precious and important to her.

Have you ever noticed how fast time seems to pass when you are doing something that you really enjoy? Many ancient people, especially the Romans, said "time flies." They used the proverb, *tempus fugit*, which means, "time flees."

When does time seem to move fast for you? Does time ever seem to "stand still?"

"Time flies when you're having fun"

my momma likes to say.
I'm not sure what she means
but I like it anyway.

I wish that I could fly with time.
I'm sure it'd be a blast!
I'd tell him when to slow it down
and when he could go fast.

"Money doesn't grow on trees,"

my momma likes to say.
I'm not sure what she means
but I like it anyway.

Just think how funny it would be
to pick a dollar from a tree.
I could not stop at picking one.
I'd pick until I had a ton!

When someone says this idiom to you, they are really saying that money is hard to come by and you have to work for it. This expression was first used in the United States in the 1750s.

What if money did grow on trees? It sounds like fun but what would we do if a tornado came along and shredded an entire crop? Or imagine a whole orchard of budding bills besieged by bugs or birds! What would we do then?

I think it's a good thing that money is made at the Bureau of Engraving and Printing in Washington, D.C. You can go there and see how it's made.

Even though it's referred to as "paper money," it is actually 75% cotton and 25% linen. Did you know that the average dollar bill lasts only 15-18 months? Do you think money would last that long if it grew on trees?

How many dollar bills do you think you could pick in one hour?
Which president's portrait appears on the dollar bill?

"Reach for the stars,"

my momma likes to say.
I'm not sure what she means
but I like it anyway.

I need to find the tallest tree
and stretch myself out far.
With just a little help
I know I'll reach a star.

 This idiom tells you to go
after the things you want. It
suggests that if you stretch your-
self mentally and physically, you will
attain your goals. Think of all the times
you stood on your tiptoes and could reach
just a little bit farther.

What do you think Ivan Sergeevich Turgenev,
a Russian author, meant when he said, "We sit
in the mud and reach for the stars."

"Love makes the world go 'round,"
my momma likes to say.
I'm not sure what she means
but I like it anyway.

Everyone should do their share
so the world will never stop.
My momma does her part
by loving me a lot.

Science tells us that gravity pulling the Earth and other planets towards the sun is what makes the world go around. This expression doesn't mock science, but is simply saying that love is what makes our lives on Earth successful and rewarding. Gravity's pull is very strong, but love, if it could be measured, is even stronger.

"Love Makes the World Go 'Round" may have been an old French song. Some people credit author Charles Dickens with first writing it down. Many songs are about love, and this saying has been used many times in song titles and lyrics.

Some people have funny ways of finishing up this proverb, by saying things like "...and so does a bump in the head," or "...but laughter keeps us from getting dizzy." Which ending do you like, or don't you like a funny ending at all?

"It's raining cats and dogs,"

my momma likes to say.
I'm not sure what she means
but I like it anyway.

Cats and dogs up in the sky?
I haven't caught one yet!
I hope that when I do
I can keep it as my pet.

 You have probably heard this idiom when it was raining really hard. It goes back to the 16th Century when "thatched" roofs, or roofs made of straw, were common. Many animals stayed on the roof to keep warm as the straw roofs retained heat. During heavy rains the straw got slippery and the animals would slide or jump off the roof and go find someplace dry to stay. Anybody looking out the window from inside the house would think that cats and dogs were falling out of the sky!

Another theory is that thunder and lightning represents a cat-and-dog fight. Or perhaps it came from mythology where a cat was thought to influence the weather and a dog was a symbol of the wind.

The next time there is a storm, imagine it's a cat and dog fight.

"Sleep tight.
Don't let the bed bugs bite,"

my momma likes to say.
I'm not sure what she means
but I like it anyway.

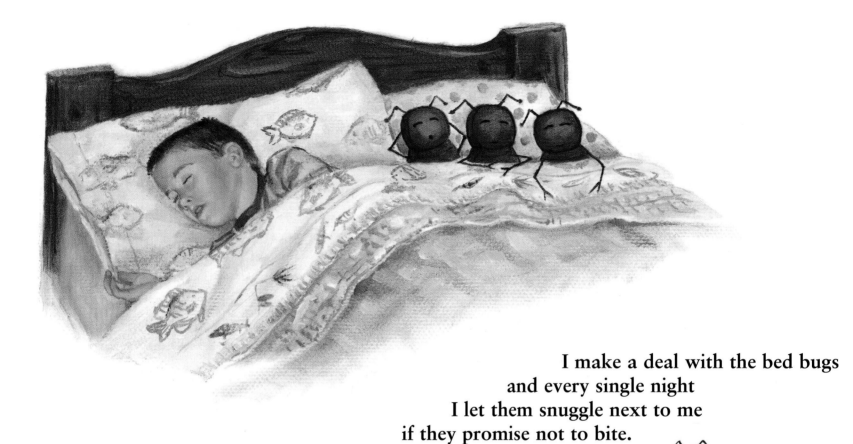

**I make a deal with the bed bugs
and every single night
I let them snuggle next to me
if they promise not to bite.**

 If you lived in the 1800s, you might have slept on a rope bed; this was a wood frame with ropes strung across to hold up the mattress. Over time the ropes would loosen, making the bed very uncomfortable. Tightening the ropes with a T-shaped tool called a bed wrench made the bed comfortable again and resulted in the expression "sleep tight."

The mattress was made up of straw, leaves, pine needles, and other things that bugs loved to munch on! So, bed bugs—a bug similar to fleas, were often found in beds and would sometimes bite.

When your momma says this to you, she is hoping that nothing will interfere with getting a good night's sleep.

What kind of deal would you make with your bed bugs? Would you let them sleep with you if they promised to make your bed in the morning?

"Cat got your tongue?"

My momma likes to say.
I'm not sure what she means
but I like it anyway.

This expression is another way of saying, "Why are you so quiet?" It was first heard and became popular in the United States and Britain in the 19th century but no one is quite sure where it originated. Some people speculate that it came about because cats are so quiet. Others think it's because if a cat really had your tongue, it would be impossible to speak.

The French have a similar saying, "I throw my tongue to the cat," meaning "I give up, I have nothing to say."

Have you ever been so quiet that someone said, "Cat got your tongue?" I don't think anyone has ever said that to me.

How long can you stretch your tongue? Can you touch your tongue to your nose?

**My cat has never tried
to take my tongue away.
But if he did he'd find that it
can stretch a long, long way.**

"If the shoe fits, wear it,"

my momma likes to say.
I'm not sure what she means
but I like it anyway.

In the 1700's people used to say, "If the cap fits, put it on." At some point, it changed to, "If the slipper fits, wear it." Maybe it changed because of the well-known story, *Cinderella*. Whether it's a cap, slipper or shoe, the meaning is the same: You should accept a statement that applies to you.

When someone says, "you are special," I hope you "wear" it!

I won't wear shoes that are too BIG
or shoes that are too small.
If it were up to me...
I wouldn't wear shoes at all!

"I have eyes in the back of my head,"

my momma likes to say.
I'm not sure what she means
but I like it anyway.

Mommas can see everything.
They have two pairs of eyes.
When you think they are not watching,
you just might be surprised!

 Does it ever seem like your momma has an extra pair of eyes?
I always thought my mom had an extra pair of eyes and some spare
ones! Having "eyes in the back of your head" means to be very alert
or to sense things without having to see them.

This idiom is very old and dates back to Roman times. It appears
in Plautus' play, *Aulularia*, written approximately 210 B.C.

How alert are you? Do you see another idiom on this page? It comes
from an Aesop fable entitled *The Milk-Woman and Her Pail*. Hint: It
means not to be overly confident of getting a result until it happens.

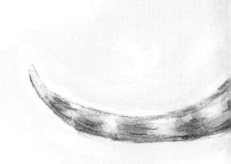

"Hold your horses,"

my momma likes to say.
I'm not sure what she means
but I like it anyway.

Momma must think I'm really strong.
Horses weigh a ton!
I'd rather have the horse hold me,
it seems a lot more fun.

 In the 1800s, a carriage driver would have to pull back on the reins to get his team of horses to slow down or stop. This was called "holding your horses." In the 1840s, this idiom was expanded to include people.

When your momma says, "hold your horses," try imagining you're a horse and some-one is pulling on your reins. Maybe it will help you slow down and be more patient.

"When life hands you lemons, make lemonade,"

my momma likes to say.
I'm not sure what she means
but I like it anyway.

If life gives me lemons
I'll squeeze them good and hard.
Then add some sugar, stir it up
and sell it from our yard.

Lemonade
25¢

Andrew Carnegie (1835-1919) first said, "When fate hands us lemons, let us try to make lemonade."

Lemons are very sour and yet they are used to make something very sweet and delicious—lemonade! This idiom suggests that we should take a difficult situation and turn it into something good.

Can you think of a time when you took a bad situation and turned it into something good?

Lemonade Recipe
2 cups granulated sugar
⅔ cup lemon peel cut in 2" x ¼ strips (about 4 lemons)
1½ cups hot water
4 cups cold water
1¼ cups lemon juice (about 8-10 lemons)

In a large pitcher, combine sugar, lemon peel and hot water. Stir until sugar dissolves. Refrigerate until very cold. Stir in cold water and lemon juice. Pour over ice to serve. Add a lemon slice.

"Laughter is the best medicine."

my momma likes to say.
I'm not sure what she means
but I like it anyway.

I sure hope momma's right
and the next time I am ill,
I'll get a dose of laughter
and not some awful pill.

 Have you ever noticed how great you feel after a good laugh?

This expression implies that laughter can take away the pain and discomfort of an illness. Realizing the medical benefits of laughter, some hospitals have clowns or humor rooms filled with comic books and funny movies, to encourage their patients to laugh.

Tell your mom and dad that laughing may be good for their hearts! A study done by cardiologists at the University of Maryland Medical Center suggests that laughter may even help minimize heart disease.

Try watching a really funny movie the next time you're sick. Your cheeks and tummy may ache from laughing, but you might discover that laughter really is the best medicine.

"I love you honey,"

my momma likes to say.
I know exactly what she means
she shows me every day.

I'm sure your momma says some special things too.

Use this page to write the things your momma says to you.

_____

_____

_____

_____

_____

_____

_____

Denise Brennan-Nelson

Home is where the heart is, and Denise Brennan-Nelson's heart and home are in Howell, Michigan. Her parents tried to *keep her feet on the ground* but she preferred to have her *head in the clouds*, which is how she discovered that *every cloud has a silver lining*.

Denise is having *the time of her life* writing for children. **My Momma Likes to Say** is her second children's book. She *got her feet wet* with **Buzzy the bumblebee**, also from Sleeping Bear Press.

Denise is *head over heels* for her husband, Bob, who is a *diamond in the rough*. They consider their daughters, Rebecca and Rachel, to be their *pride and joy*.

Jane Monroe Donovan

Jane's parents encouraged her to *follow her heart* and it led her to sketching and painting. Her talent didn't come *out of the blue*. *Practice makes perfect*, and Jane began practicing when she was *knee high to a grasshopper*.

Jane *got off to a flying start* with **Sunny Numbers: A Florida Counting Book**, also from Sleeping Bear Press. **My Momma Likes to Say** is her second children's book.

Jane's *home sweet home* is in Pinckney, Michigan with her husband, Bruce and their two sons, Ryan and Joey. Also a part of their family is Belle, their dog, and May-Lee, the cat, both of whom are featured in **My Momma Likes To Say**.

The following is a list of references the author used in her research

Ammer, Christine. 1992. *Have a Nice Day—No Problem!* New York, New York: Penguin Group/Dutton.

Mieder, Wolfgang. 1992. *Dictionary of American Proverbs*. New York: Oxford University Press.

Pine Crest School (Florida) Idiom Collection [Online, accessed 2002]. http://hray.com/idiom/

Ray House [Online, accessed 2002]. http://fhp.angelcities.com/wilsonscreek/RayHouse.html

Rogers, James. 1985. *The Dictionary of Clichés*. Avenel, NJ: Wings Books.

Terban, Marvin. 1996. *Dictionary of Idioms*. New York: Scholastic.

Washington Elementary, Fargo Public Schools, ND [Online, accessed 2002].http://www.fargo.k12.nd.us/ schools/Washington/Schutz/index.htm

Wayne Magnuson: English Idioms [Online, accessed 2002]. http://home.t-online.de/home/ toni.goeller/ idiom_wm/index.html

University of Maryland Medicine [Online, accessed 2002]. http://www.umm.edu/features/laughter.htm